0 1

menu

For Hazel, Rose and everyone at the village school in Crowhurst – B.M.

For Oliver – G.P.

PUFFIN BOOKS

Published by the Penguin Group: London, New York, Australia,
Canada, India, Ireland, New Zealand and South Africa
Penguin Books Ltd, Registered Offices:
80 Strand, London WC2R 0RL, England

puffinbooks.com

First published 2006
Published in this edition 2007
5 7 9 10 8 6 4

Manufactured in China
ISBN 978-0-140-56994-0

Trouble at the DINOSAUR CAFE

Brian Moses &

Garry Parsons

PUFFIN

Down at the Dinosaur Cafe,
everybody was doing fine.
Steggy was slurping
his swamp juice,
menu

while
Iggy
sat
down
to dine.

Patsy was eating her tree roots and had ordered vegetable pie,

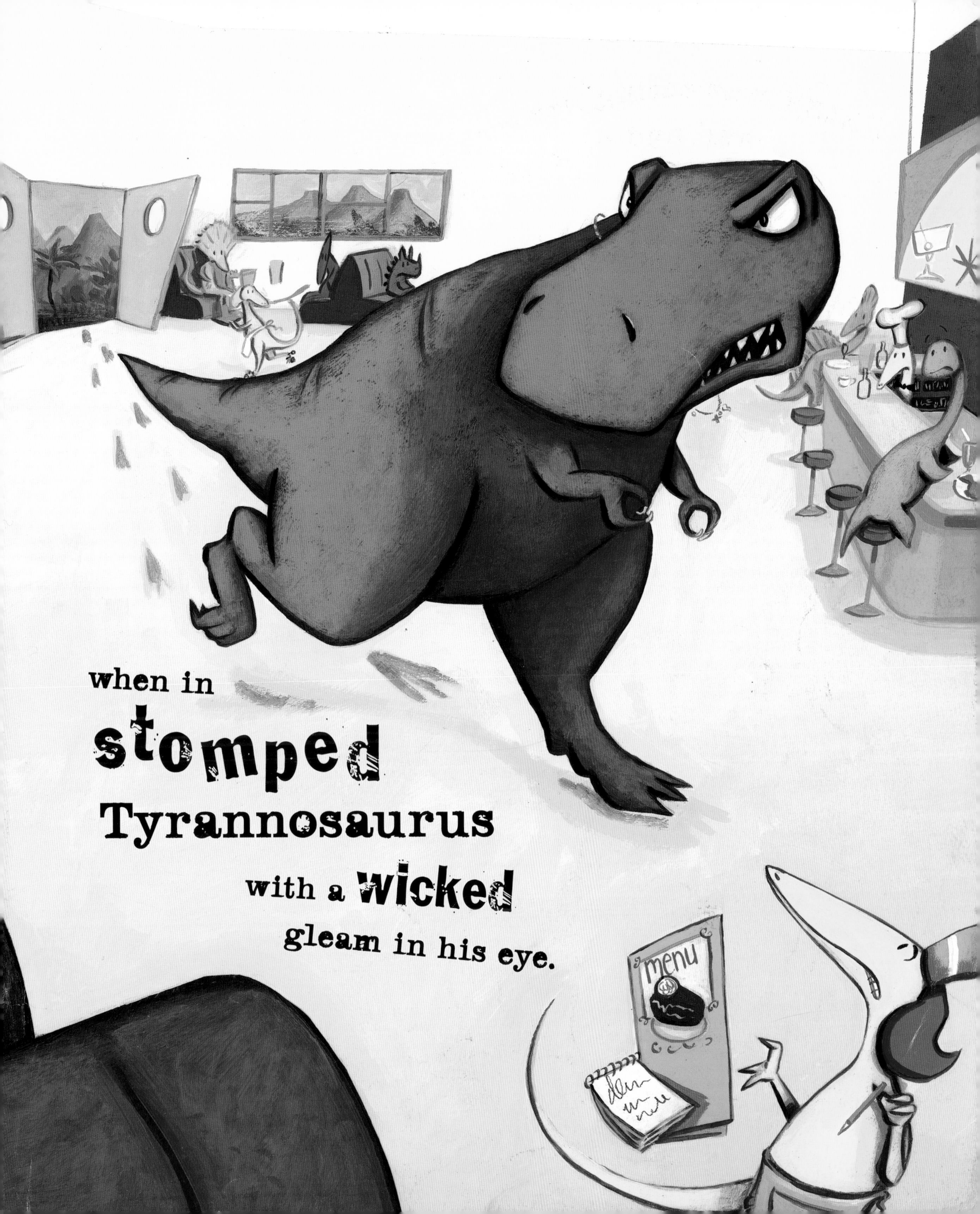
when in
stomped
Tyrannosaurus
with a wicked
gleam in his eye.
menu

He read the menu from left to right

then **gobbled** it up in one **gulp**.

He chewed upon it thoughtfully while the paper turned to pulp.

"You plant eaters are fine," he said,
"if that's all you want to eat.
But I'm a **growing** dinosaur

and my stomach **cries** out for **meat.**"

Steggy **stiffened**,

Iggy **trembled**,

while **Patsy** fell off her chair.

Tyrannosaurus turned his head

and fixed them with his **stare**:

"There's nothing I
like more," he said,
"than a **tasty dinosaur** stew,
and for extra-special flavour . . .

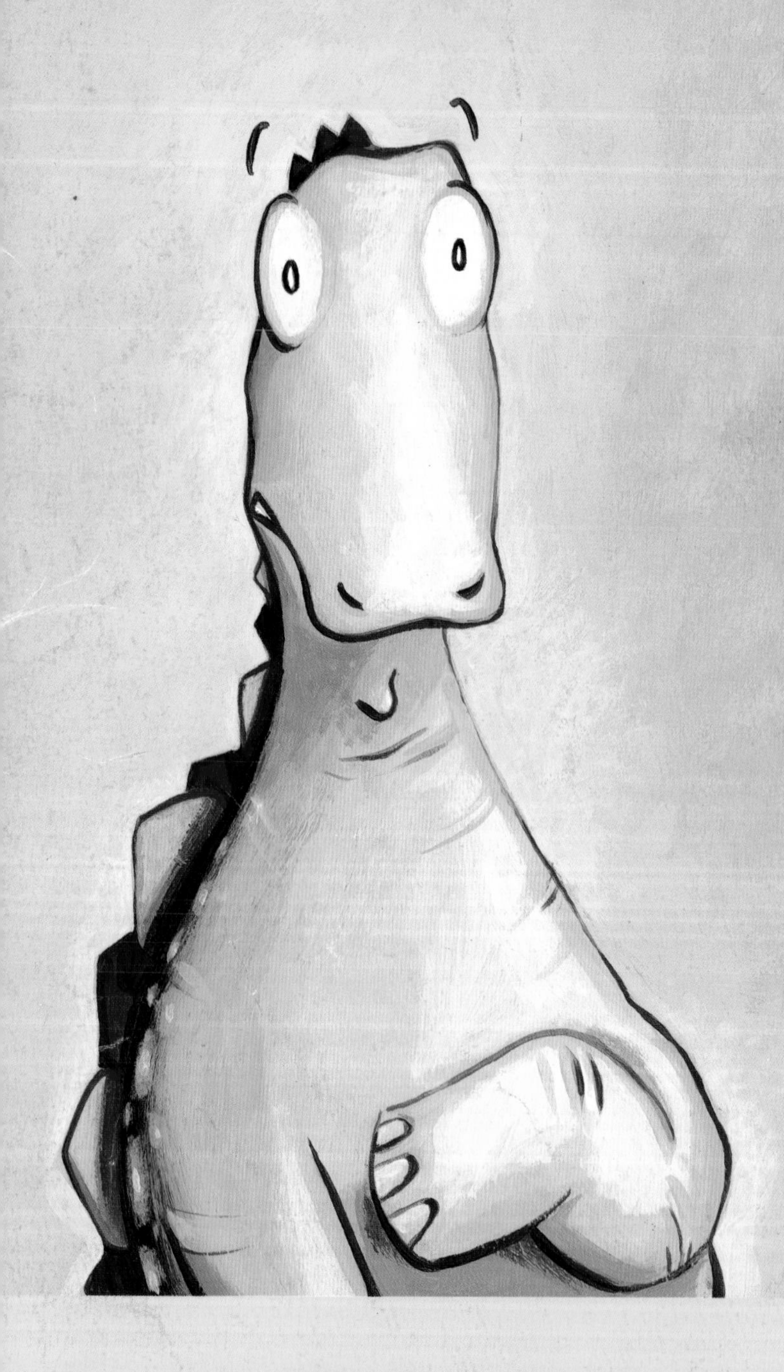

I'll add

you

and

YOU

and **YOU!"**

Then hiding behind the counter
Iggy spoke on her mobile phone:

"Terry Triceratops, please come quick,
we can't handle this on our own."

"I know what to do,"
said Terry.
"Don't worry
any more!"

He **rushed** straight round to the cafe
and **burst** in
through the door.

Terry Triceratops,
small but **deadly**,
fought Tyrannosaurus
with ease.

A whack

and a smack

from his three-pronged attack

brought the

big

bully beast

to his

knees.

Then he **knocked** him
sideways on to his back
in a move that was really neat.

Steggy and Patsy
bounced
on his tum,

while Iggy
tickled his feet.

"Stop!" he roared.
"Stop, please stop.
No more, I beg you, enough!"

"We'll stop," Steggy said,
"when you promise
that you'll stop acting so tough."

"**Anything**," wheezed Tyrannosaurus.
He was getting quite out of breath.

"And if you break that promise," warned Terry,
"we'll **tickle** you to death!"

Tyrannosaurus fled through the door
in search of easier meat,

while everyone in the Dinosaur Cafe
celebrated his defeat.

But Iggy complained to the others:
"You were OK sitting on his belly.
I had an awful time," she said . . .

"His feet were really
SMELLY!"